William Cowper, Charles Edmund Brock

The Diverting History of John Gilpin

William Cowper, Charles Edmund Brock

The Diverting History of John Gilpin

ISBN/EAN: 9783337338626

Printed in Europe, USA, Canada, Australia, Japan

Cover: Foto ©Andreas Hilbeck / pixelio.de

More available books at **www.hansebooks.com**

THE DIVERTING HISTORY of JOHN GILPIN BY WILLIAM COWPER

ILLUSTRATED BY CHAS. E BROCK

NEW YORK: E P DUTTON & CO
31 WEST TWENTY THIRD STREET
LONDON: J M DENT & CO
1899

LIST OF ILLUSTRATIONS

ON THE BALLAD OF
JOHN GILPIN

THE story of Cowper's writing of JOHN GILPIN is perhaps the gayest incident in the whole mournful record of his life. It came after his retreat to Olney under every congenial circumstance of religious melancholy. He was sunk in the native dulness of the place, which was described, more than sixty years later, as a disagreeable village surrounded by tame marshy scenery, without a hill or one romantic feature to redeem it. He was dominated by the morbid pieties of his friends the Unwins and famous Vicar of Olney, John Newton, only less miasmatic and unwholesome for one of his temperament than the marshlands which seemed their appropriate symbol. By this time too he was a man of fifty, and there seemed no chance of any natural rebound from the daily level of his depression.

Suddenly, into the midst of these dispiriting circumstances enters the sprightly figure of a lady.

Her vivacity, her dress, her natural graces, had a something unaccustomed about them, for Cowper's unsocial eyes at any rate. They came, it was rumoured in the village, of the lady's quondam residence in France. A little prestige was added, in this local gossip, by the modest title of " Lady Austen, widow of the late Sir Robert."

It might have happened that the poet, in the ordered melancholy and seclusion of his days, cloistered within the garden-walls of the Unwins' house and the adjoining Vicarage, might not have chanced on this vision of another sphere. But for once his stars were genial and auspicious. He encountered the lady casually. Then, what was an unheard-of thing for him to do, he

asked Mrs. Unwin to call upon her,—thus boldly, for the nonce,
taking his fate into his own hands. The next step was easy.
The lady moved into the quiet retreat formed by the little
Newtonian coterie. Cowper may continue this idyll in his own
words, which we borrow from one of his letters to his cousin
Lady Hesketh. Having described how Lady Austen came, in
the amiable course of these events, to take lodgings at the
Vicarage, he writes: "Between the Vicarage and the back of
our house are interposed our gardens and an orchard. She had
lived much in France, was very sensible and had infinite vivacity."
The apposition of these two simple statements easily prepares the
reader for the following step, to wit, the making of a new garden
door between the adjacent demesnes, and the rapid growth of the
acquaintance. Every morning at eleven, he tells us, "I went to
pay my devoirs to her ladyship. Customs very soon become
laws." And again: "Lady Austen and we pass our days
alternately at each other's château. In the morning I walk with

one or the other of the ladies, and in the evening wind thread."

This recalls inevitably the descriptions in *The Task* of the "Winter Morning's Walk" and the "Winter Evening"; for *The Task* was, as we know, directly inspired by Lady Austen. They do not give us as many of those particular glimpses of life at Olney, which most interest us now, as we could wish; but the vigorous pictorial opening lines of the "Winter Evening" work themselves naturally and with much warmth of colouring into the picture. A subsequent passage recalls in Cowper's particular vein of amiable, half-feminine fireside reminiscence the scene, with the poet winding thread or reading aloud, while the ladies sewed and listened, or sang; and Lady Austen, we doubt, rallied her half-humorous, half-melancholy admirer.

> " *The poet's or historian's page by one*
> *Made vocal for th' amusement of the rest;*
> *The sprightly lyre, whose treasure of sweet sounds*

OF JOHN GILPIN

The touch from many a trembling chord shakes out ;
And the clear voice symphonious, yet distinct,
And in the charming strife triumphant still,
Beguile the night, and set a keener edge
On female industry : the threaded steel
Flies swiftly, and unfelt the task proceeds.
The volume clos'd, the customary rites
Of the last meal commence."

It was in one such evening that Lady Austen told Cowper, incidentally to those topics in which she excelled and to which he refers, "dangers escaped, foes disappointed, life preserved and peace restored," the diverting history of John Gilpin. It delighted him beyond words. He, the melancholy poet, fairly roared, we are told, over the delicious misfortunes of the road, which were now recollected, now invented, by the witty narrator. What is most significant of all, he spent a sleepless night in turning the story into a ballad. The ballad seems to have attained a fame in

MS. forthwith ; that it charmed the little circle, where it had its first beginnings, need hardly be explained. Its first public appearance was in the columns of the *Public Advertiser;* and thereafter its success was enormous. Henderson the actor recited it to crowds of people in London. It was copied, quoted, pirated, published and republished. Lady Austen, in a word, had converted, by one witty story wittily told, the sombre recluse of Olney into a popular poet.

She soon disappeared again from his shy orbit. The ladies of Olney, perhaps not unnaturally, resented her Gallic sprightliness and her gradual absorption of their chief luminary. Moreover, the airs of the marshes did not agree with her. So she went, as she had come. There was a little correspondence, broken off by the poet's recurring mood of other-worldliness, mixed perhaps with social prudence. And that was all.

Still, let us remember that, save for Lady Austen, we should not have had the major part of those things that keep Cowper's name alive to-day.   It was she who suggested *The Task* ; she who prompted the noble Royal George lines.   Above all, since that is here our immediate concern, to her and her alone we owe it, as we have told, that the DIVERTING HISTORY OF JOHN GILPIN was ever written.

Mr. Brock's congenially devised illustrations, for the rest, form a better appreciation of the ballad and its humours than any commentary the critic is likely to offer.

ERNEST RHYS.

The Diverting History of JOHN GILPIN

I

JOHN GILPIN was a citizen
 Of credit and renown,
A train-band Captain eke was he
 Of famous London town.

II

JOHN GILPIN'S spouse said to her dear,

"Though wedded we have been

These twice ten tedious years, yet we

No holiday have seen.

III

"TO-MORROW is our wedding-day,

And we will then repair

Unto the Bell at Edmonton,

All in a chaise and pair.

"To-morrow is
  our wedding day"

" MY sister and my sister's child,

Myself and children three,

Will fill the chaise, so you must ride

On horseback after we."

HE soon replied, "I do admire

Of womankind but one,

And you are she, my dearest dear,

Therefore it shall be done.

VI

"I AM a linendraper bold,

    As all the world doth know,

And my good friend the calender

    Will lend his horse to go."

VII

QUOTH Mrs. Gilpin, "That's well said;

    And for that wine is dear,

We will be furnish'd with our own,

    Which is both bright and clear."

VIII

JOHN GILPIN kiss'd his loving wife ;
    O'erjoy'd was he to find
That, though on pleasure she was bent,
    She had a frugal mind.

IX

THE morning came, the chaise was brought,
    But yet was not allow'd
To drive up to the door, lest all
    Should say that she was proud.

X

SO three doors off the chaise was stay'd,
　　Where they did all get in,
Six precious souls, and all agog
　　To dash through thick and thin.

XI

SMACK went the whip, round went the wheels,
　　Were never folk so glad,
The stones did rattle underneath
　　As if Cheapside were mad.

"Where they
did all get in"

XII

JOHN GILPIN at his horse's side
  Seized fast the flowing mane,
And up he got in haste to ride,
  But soon came down again ;

XIII

FOR saddle-tree scarce reach'd had he,
  His journey to begin,
When, turning round his head, he saw
  Three customers come in.

XIV

SO down he came : for loss of time,
 Although it grieved him sore,
Yet loss of pence, full well he knew,
 Would trouble him much more.

XV

'TWAS long before the customers
 Were suited to their mind,
When Betty screaming came down stairs,
 "The wine is left behind!"

...ing before the customers
Were suited to their mind

"GOOD lack !" quoth he—"yet bring it me,

My leathern belt likewise,

In which I bear my trusty sword

When I do exercise."

XVII

NOW Mistress Gilpin, careful soul !

Had two stone bottles found,

To hold the liquor that she loved,

And keep it safe and sound.

XVIII

EACH bottle had a curling ear,

  Through which the belt he drew,

And hung a bottle on each side

  To make his balance true.

XIX

THEN over all, that he might be

  Equipp'd from top to toe,

His long red cloak, well brush'd and neat,

  He manfully did throw.

"Equipped from top to toe"

XX

NOW see him mounted once again
Upon his nimble steed,
Full slowly pacing o'er the stones
With caution and good heed.

XXI

BUT finding soon a smoother road
  Beneath his well-shod feet,
The snorting beast began to trot,
  Which gall'd him in his seat.

XXII

"SO, fair and softly," John he cried.
  But John he cried in vain;
That trot became a gallop soon,
  In spite of curb and rein.

"The snorting beast began to trot"

XXIII

SO stooping down, as needs he must
    Who cannot sit upright,
He grasp'd the mane with both his hands,
    And eke with all his might.

XXIV

HIS horse, who never in that sort
    Had handled been before,
What thing upon his back had got
    Did wonder more and more.

XXV

AWAY went Gilpin, neck or nought,

    Away went hat and wig,

He little dreamt when he set out,

    Of running such a rig.

"At last
it flew away"

XXVI

THE wind did blow, the cloak did fly,
  Like streamer long and gay,
Till loop and button failing both,
  At last it flew away.

XXVII

THEN might all people well discern
  The bottles he had slung,
A bottle swinging at each side,
  As hath been said or sung.

XXVIII

THE dogs did bark, the children scream'd,
  Up flew the windows all,
And ev'ry soul cried out " Well done ! "
  As loud as he could bawl.

XXIX

AWAY went Gilpin—who but he !
  His fame soon spread around,—
He carries weight ! he rides a race !
  'Tis for a thousand pound !

XXX

AND still as fast as he drew near,
　　'Twas wonderful to view
How in a trice the turnpike-men
　　Their gates wide open threw.

XXXI

AND now as he went bowing down
His reeking head full low,

The bottles twain behind his back

Were shatter'd at a blow.

XXXII

DOWN ran the wine into the road
Most piteous to be seen,

Which made his horse's flanks to smoke

As they had basted been.

"The bottles twain behind his back
Were shattered at a blow"

XXXIII

BUT still he seem'd to carry weight,
　　With leathern girdle braced,
For all might see the bottle necks
　　Still dangling at his waist.

XXXIV

THUS all through merry Islington
　　These gambols he did play,
Until he came unto the wash
　　Of Edmonton so gay.

XXXV

AND there he threw the wash about
On both sides of the way,

Just like unto a trundling mop,
Or a wild-goose at play.

XXXVI

AT Edmonton his loving wife
From the balcony spied

Her tender husband, wond'ring much
To see how he did ride.

34

XXXVII

"STOP, stop John Gilpin!—Here's the
house!"
They all at once did cry;
"The dinner waits, and we are tir'd."
Said Gilpin—"So am I!"

XXXVIII

BUT yet his horse was not a whit
Inclined to tarry there;
For why?—his owner had a house
Full ten miles off at Ware.

XXXIX

So like an arrow swift he flew
   Shot by an archer strong ;
So did he fly—which brings me to
   The middle of my song.

XL

Away went Gilpin, out of breath,
   And sore against his will,
Till at his friend the calender's
   His horse at last stood still.

XLI

THE calender, amazed to see

His neighbour in such trim,

Laid down his pipe, flew to the gate,

And thus accosted him:

37

XLII

"WHAT news? what news? your tidings tell,

   Tell me you must and shall—

Say why bareheaded you are come,

   Or why you come at all?"

XLIII

NOW Gilpin had a pleasant wit,

   And loved a timely joke,

And thus unto the calender

   In merry guise he spoke:

"What news? what news?
your tidings tell"

XLIV

"I CAME because your horse would come,
  And if I well forbode,
My hat and wig will soon be here,
  They are upon the road."

XLV

THE calender, right glad to find
  His friend in merry pin,
Return'd him not a single word,
  But to the house went in ;

WHENCE straight he came with hat and
    wig,
  A wig that flow'd behind,
A hat not much the worse for wear,
  Each comely in its kind.

HE held them up, and in his turn
  Thus show'd his ready wit :
" My head is twice as big as yours,
  They therefore needs must fit.

"BUT let me scrape the dirt away
That hangs upon your face;
And stop and eat, for well you may
Be in a hungry case."

SAID John, "It is my wedding-day,
And all the world would stare,
If wife should dine at Edmonton,
And I should dine at Ware."

L

SO turning to his horse, he said,
  "I am in haste to dine,
'Twas for your pleasure you came here,
  You shall go back for mine."

LI

AH, luckless speech, and bootless boast !
  For which he paid full dear,
For while he spake a braying ass
  Did sing most loud and clear ;

"A braying ass
Did sing most loud and clear."

LII

WHEREAT his horse did snort, as he
　　Had heard a lion roar,
And gallop'd off with all his might,
　　As he had done before.

LIII

AWAY went Gilpin, and away
　　Went Gilpin's hat and wig;
He lost them sooner than at first,
　　For why?—they were too big.

LIV

NOW Mistress Gilpin, when she saw
Her husband posting down
Into the country far away,
She pull'd out half-a-crown ;

LV

AND thus unto the youth she said,
That drove them to the Bell,
"This shall be yours when you bring back
My husband safe and well."

LVI

THE youth did ride, and soon did meet

John coming back amain,

Whom in a trice he tried to stop

By catching at his rein ;

45

BUT not performing what he meant,
    And gladly would have done,
The frighted steed he frighted more,
    And made him faster run.

LVIII

AWAY went Gilpin, and away
    Went post-boy at his heels,
The post-boy's horse right glad to miss
    The lumb'ring of the wheels.

"Stop thief! stop thief!
a highwayman!"

LIX

SIX gentlemen upon the road
  Thus seeing Gilpin fly,
With post-boy scampering in the rear,
  They rais'd the hue and cry :

LX

"STOP thief! stop thief!—a highwayman !"
  Not one of them was mute ;
And all and each that pass'd that way
  Did join in the pursuit.

LXI

A ND now the turnpike gates again

    Flew open in short space,

The toll-men thinking as before

    That Gilpin rode a race.

"For he got first
to Town"

LXII

A ND so he did, and won it too,

For he got first to town,

Nor stopp'd till where he had got up

He did again get down.

G210998

LXIII

NOW let us sing, Long live the king,

And Gilpin long live he:

And when he next doth ride abroad,

May I be there to see!

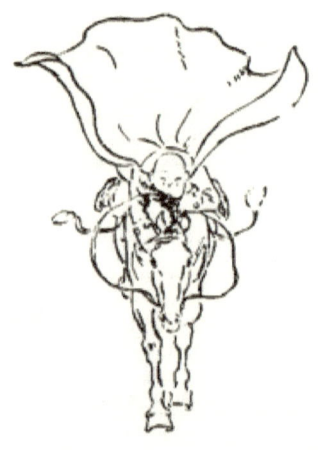

Printed by BALLANTYNE, HANSON & Co.
London & Edinburgh

www.ingramcontent.com/pod-product-compliance
Lightning Source LLC
Chambersburg PA
CBHW032345020726
47499CB00009B/3177